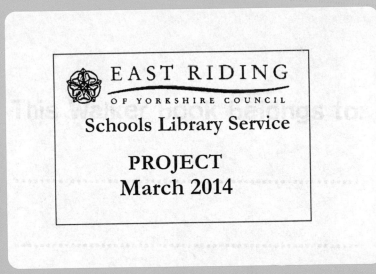

First published 2010 by Walker Books Ltd

87 Vauxhall Walk, London SE11 5HJ

This edition published 2011

2 4 6 8 10 9 7 5 3 1

This book has been typeset in Imperfect

Printed in China

British Library Cataloguing in Publication Data:

a catalogue record for this book is available from the British Library

ISBN 978-1-4063-3193-6

www.walker.co.uk

WALKER BOOKS

AND SUBSIDIARIES

LONDON · BOSTON · SYDNEY · AUCKLAND

SPECKLE

the

SPIDER

Emma Dodson

Speckle the spider loved to dance. He was always prancing about in front of his friends at school. But his showing off would get him in trouble with Miss Tarantula, the teacher.

SPECKLE! SPIN that silk, don't SKIP with it!

SUNNYSIDE SCHOOL

SUNNYSIDE SCHOOL FOR SPIDERS

SCHOOL REPORT

But Speckle
couldn't help himself.
I'm sure I'm a very special
sort of spider, he thought.

One day, Speckle got a
tiny little letter from his tiny
little friend, Mr Flip Flap the flea.

Hey Speckle,
How are your bananas hanging?
Look at me on this flyer. I've
joined the world-famous Fabulous
Flying Flea Circus. People go crazy
for us.

Love from

Flip Flap

If people love Mr Flip Flap's flying,
they will really love my dancing,
thought Speckle. I must show
the world how special I am!

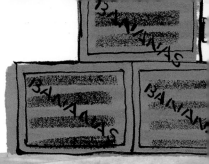

So Speckle teamed up with a bunch of bananas and set sail in search of fame.

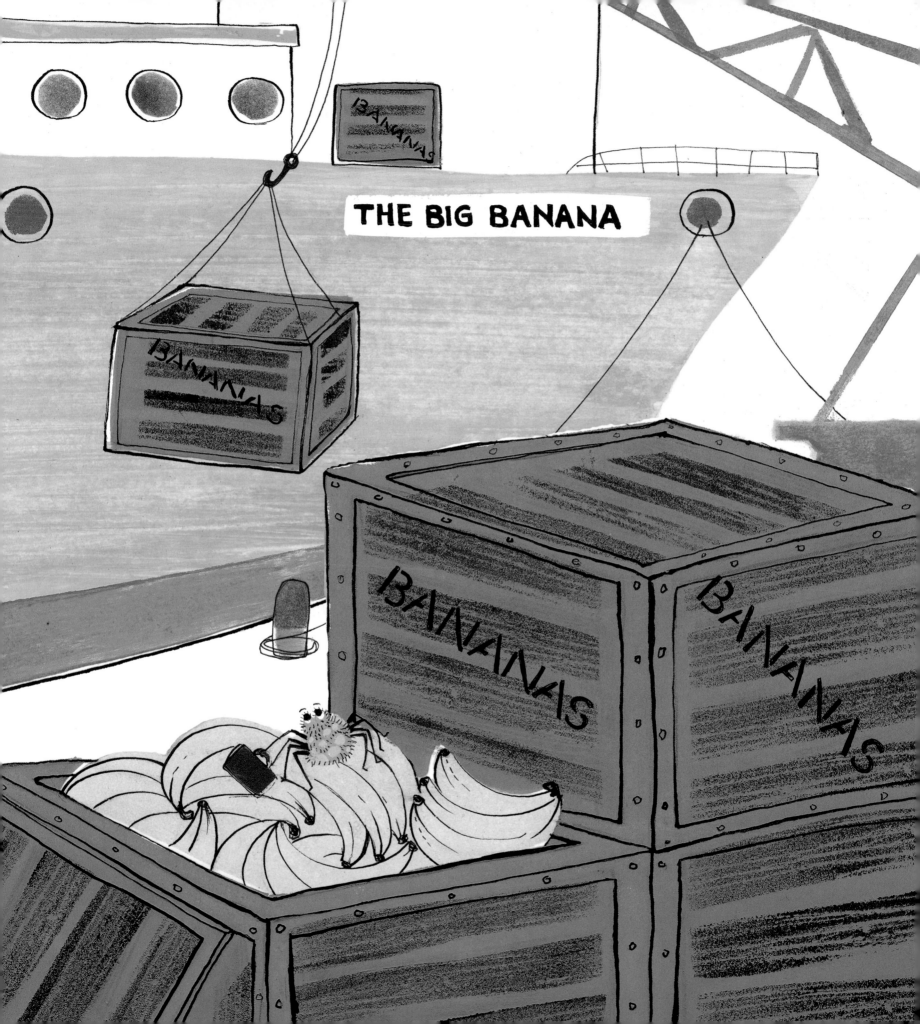

After a long journey,
Speckle and the bananas
finally arrived at their new home.
Speckle began to explore.

Suddenly he noticed a great
big furry giant watching him.
"Hello," said Speckle. "Would you
like to see my razzle dazzle dance?"
And he started to tap his toes.

The great big furry giant

HISSED

and

HUFFED.

Then it poked Speckle **really** hard
with the sharp bits on the end of its leg.

Speckle ran and
hid in his bananas.

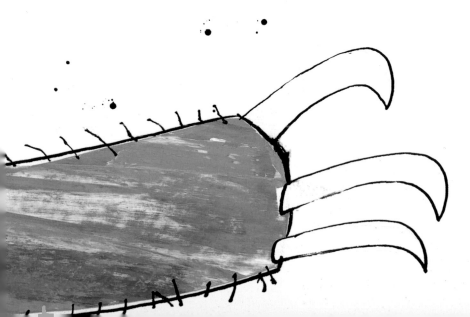

The next day, Speckle peeped
out and found an enormous
pink monster staring at him.

"Hello," said Speckle.
"Do you want to see
what a special spider I am?"
And he started to wiggle his feet.

Then several terrible things happened.

"OWWWWW!"

He was walloped
on the backside
very hard ...

"WHOOOAHH!"

sent skidding at
top speed ...

"WEEEEOO!"

flying, falling ... really fast ...

until he knew
that now he
needed to run
instead of dance.

Investigation of spider

by Harry Highbottom

Speckle eventually found himself a big white place to hide in.
Suddenly there was the most terrifying noise
Speckle had ever heard.
It sounded like ...

AAAARGH!
THERE'S A
HUGE SPIDER
IN THE BATH!!

bubble
bath

Speckle **squeezed** himself down a handy hole.

It was dark, wet, smelly and scary

but Speckle slid and slipped along as fast as he could

until at last he saw daylight.

He headed towards it ...

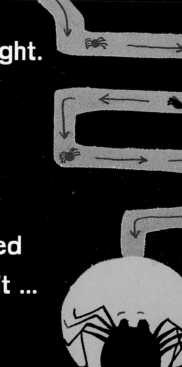

and found lots of giant
eyes staring at him.
Speckle gulped.
"Hello," he said. "I'm special!"

But before he could start
his dance he felt himself
being lifted through the air.

Oh, no,
thought Speckle.
Then it went
completely dark.

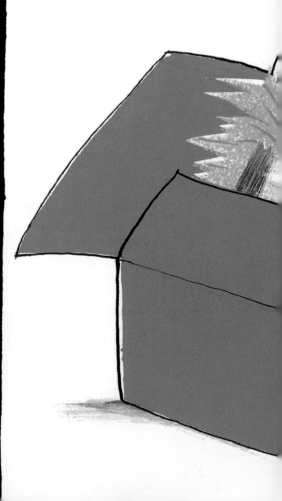

SPECKLY SPIDER

The Daily Snail

Everyday the same   Very cheap newspaper 20p

LOTS OF **FREE** STUFF INSIDE

Rare spider spotted in Surbiton

By Wally Worm

Mrs Helena Highbottom of 123 Poshmans Crescent spotted this rare, exotic (non-poisonous) spider in her bath yesterday morning.

"I was a bit scared when I saw it sitting in my bathroom. It ran down the plughole but my clever daughter Hettie caught it in an empty marmalade jar as it was trying to escape out of the kitchen sink."

Continued on page 8

Continued on page 8

The next morning Speckle was on the
front page of all the newspapers.
Wow! thought Speckle.
I knew I was special. Now I can
show everyone my dancing.

The Daily Bellylaugh

FREE
DVD

SPIDERS IN SPACE

"A brilliant movi
with lots of flashy
special effects."

...ssor Knowitall

...ckly spider

Speckly spider in the bath

By Anthony Anthill
"We think the almost
extinct arachnid
must have travelled
all the way from
the Bahamas," said
Professor Knowitall
from the Spider
University. "The
...ly other known
...er of this

kind in the country
lives at Wiffsnail Zoo.
Her name is 'Stunner'
Suzy. We intend to let
the two spiders meet,
just to see if they get
along."

...ONOUS?

...sonous.

...isonous spider
...n often be found
...eat.

THE
SUD

Speckle was given a lovely home
at the zoo, where he met Suzy.
Although Suzy couldn't dance as
well as Speckle, she could do
a pretty good somersault.

Every day thousands of people came to the zoo just to see him and Suzy. Speckle got lots of fan mail and loved being the most special spider in the country.

To Speckle and Suzy zoo

SPECKLE THE SP
SPIDER DEPAR
WIFFSN

drawn by Kayleigh
age 4¾

Love and Kisses
From
Kayleigh, KYLIE
X and keeley XX

Then one day Speckle felt he had had enough of being stared at all day long. It was hard work being the most special spider in the country. He and Suzy decided to run away.

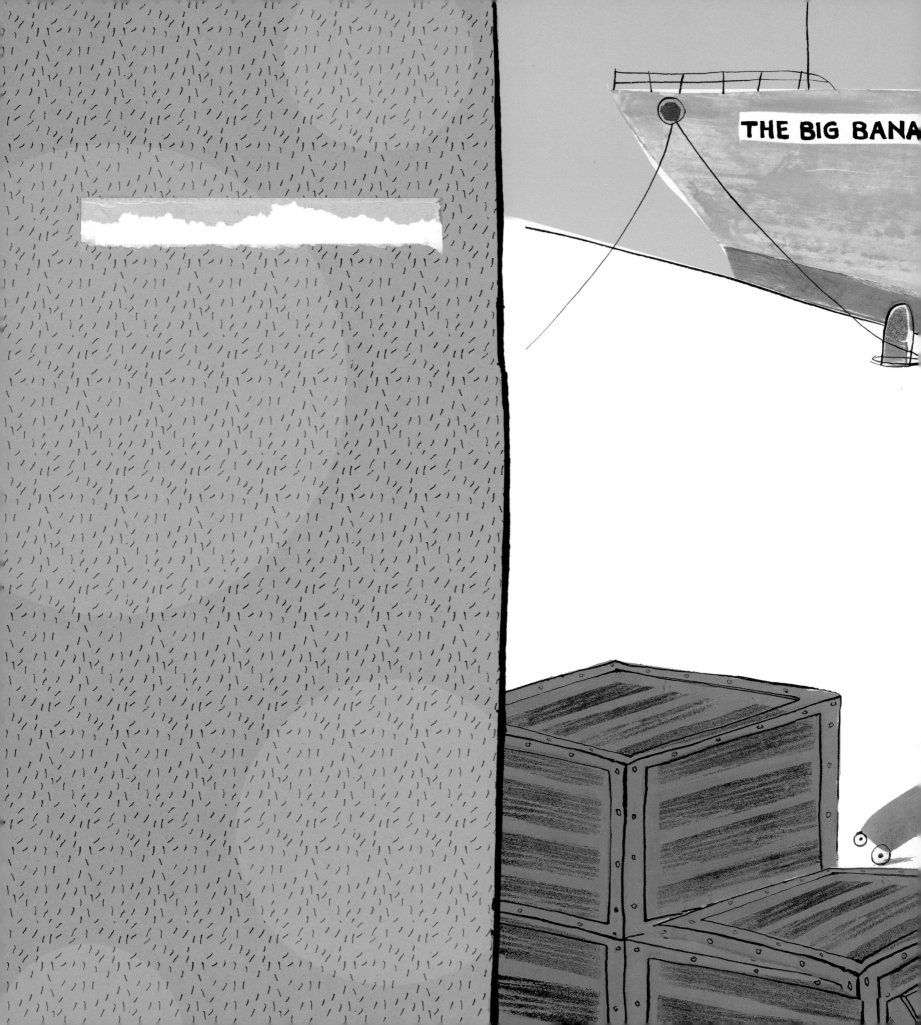

THE BIG BANA

Although there was a national search for
the superstar spiders, they were never found.
While everyone was looking for them,
Speckle and Suzy were making their way …

back to the Bahamas!

Speckle realized it wasn't
the cameras and fan mail that
made him feel special any more.

It was his
family and friends!

Spider Facts

1. Spiders have as many as eight eyes.

2. Despite having eight eyes most spiders can't see very well and have to use the hairs on their body to feel their way around.

3. Spiders have 48 knees!

4. A spider might take up to twelve hours to finish eating a big, juicy fly!

5. There are more than 40,000 different species of spider (only one of which is vegetarian).

6. Apparently, fried spiders taste like nuts... Yuk!

7. The smallest spider in the world is so tiny that you could fit ten of them on the end of a pencil!

8. The biggest is the giant huntsman, which can grow up to 30cm.

9. Most spiders live for about a year, but some tarantulas have been known to live for more than 25 years.

10. Spider silk is as strong as steel.